This book belongs to

....

If you like practicing to read,
here is a little treat:
there are lots of stories to be told
right here on Sticker Street!

Copyright © 2015

make believe ideas ltd

The Wilderness, Berkhamsted, Hertfordshire, HP4 2AZ, UK.
501 Nelson Place, P.O. Box 141000, Nashville, TN 37214-1000, USA.

www.makebelieveideas.com

·STICKER STREET·

PIP'S PLAYFUL PETS

Written by Hayley Down

Illustrated by Stuart Lynch

make
believe
ideas

READING TOGETHER

This book is an ideal first reader for your child, combining simple words and sentences with beautiful illustrations. Here are some of the many ways you can help your child with early steps in reading.

Encourage your child to:

- Look at and explore the detail in the pictures.
- Sound out the letters in each word.
- Read and repeat each short sentence.

Look at rhymes

Encourage your child to recognize rhyming words.
Try asking the following questions:

- What does this word say?
- Can you find a word that rhymes with it?
- Look at the ending of two words that rhyme. Are they spelled the same? For example, "box" and "fox," "store" and "floor."

Test understanding

After your child has read the book, try different activities to make sure that he or she has understood the text:

- Play "find the mistake." Read the text as your child looks at the words with you, but make an obvious mistake to see if he or she notices. Then ask your child to correct you.
- Make up questions to ask your child.
- Ask your child whether a statement is true or false.

Playful Pets stickers

At the corner of every page there is an area for your child to place a sticker. Help your child to build confidence and enjoy reading by celebrating when they finish a page.

What happens next?

This activity encourages children to retell the story and point to the mixed-up pictures in the right order.

Playful Pets quiz

These pages contain a simple quiz. Ask the questions and see if your child can remember the right answers from the text. If not, encourage him or her to look up the answers.

Key words

These pages provide practice with very common words used in the context of the book. Read the sentences with your child and encourage him or her to make up more sentences using the key words listed around the border.

Picture dictionary

Ask your child to look carefully at each word, cover it with his or her hand, write it on a separate piece of paper, and finally, check it!

Do not complete all the activities at once – doing one each time you read will ensure that your child continues to enjoy the story and the time you are spending together.

Have fun!

On Sticker Street, Pip's Playful Pets
is full of fuzzy friends.
They laugh together all day long
until the store day ends.

One morning something strange appears:
a big box on the floor!
The creatures wonder who's inside –
who's come to join their store?

I have read these pages.

So Peter Puppy goes to sniff
around the big brown box.

"I smell sharp claws!" he woofs with fear.
"I think it is a fox!"

Next it's Kitty's turn to try.
She takes a look inside.

"It has big ears, just like a bear!"
She mews, "It's time to hide!"

I have read these pages.

"No pet is scarier than me!"
hisses Python Brian.

But when he peeps inside the box,
he thinks he sees a lion!

I have read these pages.

Then Polly Parrot flies around
to take a little peek.

"I see a monster!" Polly squawks.
"It has a big, sharp beak!"

15

The animals are terrified –
they all shiver with fright!
But Peter Puppy has a plan
to make everything right:

"However big the creature is,
we will not need to hide
if we all go look together
to find out what's inside!"

I have read these pages

17

So all together, safe and sound,
they peer inside the box.

It doesn't hold a lion,
bear, monster, or fox . . .

I have read these pages.

19

The pet they find is soft and small,
and cuddly as can be!

"It's a mouse!" they all cry out.
The mouse squeaks, "Don't hurt me!"

The pets all laugh and tell the mouse,
"Hooray! Let's make amends!"
The little mouse feels right at home
and soon they're all great friends.

I have read these pages.

But suddenly a new surprise
arrives at the front door.

24

Now it's your turn to take a guess!
Who's next to join the store?

this
way
UP

•WHAT HAPPENS NEXT?•

Some of the pictures from the story have been mixed up! Can you retell the story and point to each picture in the correct order?

· PLAYFUL PETS QUIZ ·

Read the statements and then
decide if they are true or false.

1. Peter Puppy thought a fox was in the box.

True.

2. Kitty went to bed.

False.

3. The python's name is Brian.

True.

4. Polly Parrot ate some seeds.

False.

5. The animals found
   a bear in the box.

False.

6. The animals found
   a mouse in the box.

True.

7. The mouse was angry.

False.

KEY WORDS

Here are some key words used in context. Help your child to use other words from the border in simple sentences.

Peter Puppy **is** scared.

Kitty thinks **she** sees a bear.

I ☆ up ☆ could ☆ we ☆ yes ☆ and ☆
no it see she me of in come
the ☆ am ☆ all ☆ don't ☆ my ☆

on ☆ at ☆ for ☆ a ☆ are ☆ some

Polly Parrot
flies **up** high.

The box **doesn't**
hold a lion.

The mouse is
small and soft.

The animals all **make** friends.

☆ you ☆ when ☆ this ☆ make ☆ they ☆ were ☆ is

big ☆ has ☆ what ☆ he ☆ doesn't ☆

· PICTURE DICTIONARY ·

box

door

fox

friends

monster

mouse

parrot

puppy

python